THE LITTLE MERMAID

King Triton's daughter Ariel wants to be a part of the human world. Her friend, a crab called Sebastian, begs her to see all the great things about living under the sea. Do you see these fish and instruments Sebastian is using to make his point?

Now try these!

Kettle drum

Accordion

Bagpipes

Tuba

Triangle

Guitar

Tambourine

Harmonica

Violin

Beginners

THE LITTLE MERMAID

Ariel has a secret hideaway where she keeps treasures from the human world. Her friend Scuttle has told her all about the different things humans use. Can you find some of them in Ariel's grotto?

HERMIT CRAB KEEP OUT!

Beginners

- Mirror
- Top
- Silver platter

Now try these!

- Birdcage
- Baby bottle
- Piggy bank

- Spinning wheel
- Ice skates
- Scissors

Disney PRINCESS

THE LITTLE MERMAID

Ariel is finally a human! But the human world is a strange place. It is everything she hoped it would be — and more. Look around the castle walls for these members of Prince Eric's kingdom who can't wait to meet Ariel.

Beginners

Now try these!

◆ Juggler

◆ Carriage driver

◆ Cart seller

◆ Waiter

◆ Farmer and his horse

◆ Three men in a tub

◆ Woodcutter

◆ Police officers

◆ Fishmonger

THE LITTLE MERMAID

One kiss. That's all it will take to save Ariel from Ursula's evil spell. The lagoon is alive with music as everyone awaits the magical moment. Look in and around the water for these creatures watching the romantic evening unfold.

Now try these!

- Mama duck and her ducklings
- Crooning flamingoes
- Turtle parade
- Shell-balancing seal
- Very strong chipmunks
- Conducting porcupine
- "Love" birds forming a heart
- Lizard soloist
- Leap frogs

Beginners

THE LITTLE MERMAID

Wish Eric and Ariel *bon voyage* as the sun sets on their wedding day! It is a celebration like none ever seen on land or under the sea. First look for these friends who have come to say good-bye to the couple, then see if you can spot some wedding "bells" at the celebration!

Now try these!

◇ Ariel, the belle of the ball
◇ Belly flop
◇ Blue bell
◇ Bell-bottoms
◇ Barbells
◇ Belly laugh
◇ Dinner bell
◇ Bell pepper

Beginners

Cinderella

Cinderella is thrilled with the dress her little friends have made for her! In addition to the pretty pink frock, the mice and birds also came up with these creations. Can you find these dresses and accessories in Cinderella's tower bedroom?

Beginners

Now try these!

Pearl necklace

Long orange dress

Black shoes

Cowboy boots

Hoop skirt

Top hat

Chef's hat

Artist's beret

Bloomers

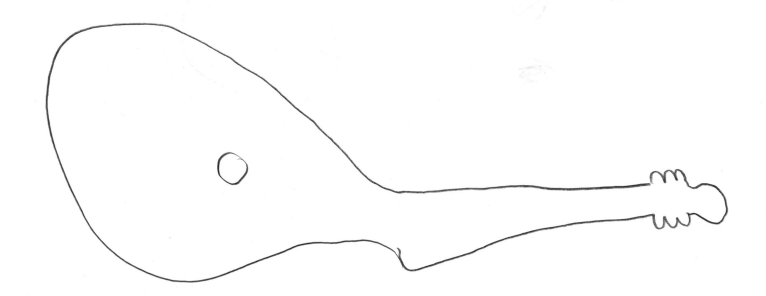

Cinderella

Cinderella's stepsisters ruined her dress, but the Fairy Godmother has arrived to save the day! Look around the garden for these things she will need to complete the transformation. Then search for these creatures that are so excited for Cinderella's big night.

Now try these!

A yellow butterfly

Bunny

Skunks

The deer family

Helpful bluebirds

A line of ants

Squirrel

Brown snail

Bullfrog

Beginners

Cinderella

At midnight, Cinderella will lose a glass slipper. But some other maidens have already lost their accessories! Can you find these ladies searching for what they've misplaced? Then look around the ball for the pieces they have lost.

Beginners

Now try these!

Purple fan

Pink cloak

Blue earring

Green pocketbook

Yellow glove

Black pocket watch

Red necklace

Silver tiara

Orange bow

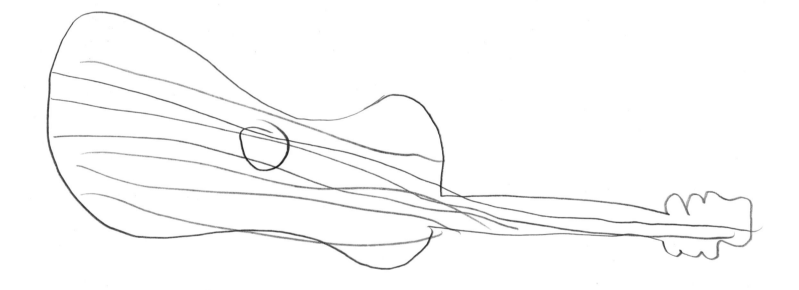

Beauty and the Beast

It's a hustle-bustle morning in the village, and Belle is off to visit the bookstore — again. First find Belle. Then look around the town square for these villagers who don't understand Belle's passion for books. And then see if you can spot some characters who seem to love reading as much as Belle does!

Now try these!

Nursemaid reading *Mother Goose*

Girl reading *Cinderella*

Belle figurine for sale

Boy reading a diary

Cook reading a cookbook

Frog reading *The Frog Prince*

Sheep enjoying a new book

Bats with a book in their belfry

The bookseller

Beginners

Beauty and the Beast

Belle's father, Maurice, has been busy in his workshop. He has invented some things that were ahead of their time. Belle knows her father is a genius, but she wonders what some of these contraptions are supposed to do. Can you find some of Maurice's wacky inventions in his workshop?

Now try these!

- Bubble machine
- Ceiling shoes
- Automatic hair cutter
- Handwritten typewriter
- Bread slicer
- Self-pouring teapot
- Fan
- Fire extinguisher
- Doorbell system

Beginners

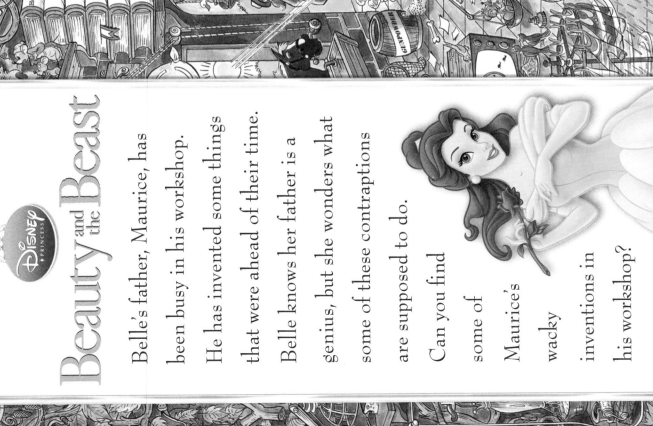

Beauty and the Beast

The Beast has everything a man or beast could desire, but he isn't happy. He hopes Belle will fall in love with him and break the spell that turned him into a beast. His enchanted servants hope so, too. Can you find some of them here in the castle? How about these other bewitched items?

Beginners

- Bucket
- Jump-roping knight
- Knitting chair
- Self-stirring pot
- Broom and dustpan
- Watering can

Now try these!

- Dueling swords
- Ladder
- Perfume bottle

Beauty and the Beast

Belle doesn't have much
of an appetite tonight, but
Mrs. Potts and Lumiere are
sure they can tempt her to try
just a tiny bite of something.
Perhaps a little music will
help. Can you find these
tempting morsels
that the kitchen
has whipped up
for Belle's first
supper in
the castle?

Now try these!

Bowl of cherries   Pancake   Vegetable basket

Sliced roast   Kabobs   Heart-shaped cookie

Punch   Gravy boat   Sandwich

Beginners

Beauty and the Beast

Gaston wants to get rid of the Beast and marry Belle, so he leads a mob of villagers to the Beast's castle. But the castle's residents won't let them through without a fight! Look around for these brave soldiers defending the Beast's home.

Beginners

Now try these!

Wardrobe

Bearskin rug

Knitting needles

Furnace

Broom

Ax

Bookcase

Desk

Trumpet

Beauty and the Beast

The Beast was not the only enchanted person living in the castle. When Belle helped turn the Beast back into a prince, the servants were transformed, too. Do you see these familiar faces in their human forms? Then look for these delicacies they've set out for the celebration.

Beginners

Now try these!

Roast pig

Ice sculpture

Wheel of cheese

Bread basket

Spaghetti

Gelatin creation

Soup

Bundt cake

Basket of oranges

Sleeping Beauty

It's no wonder the good fairies had to use their magic to make Briar Rose's birthday cake. Just look at the mess they made trying to bake without their wands! Then see if you can find these things that are making the party planning so festive.

Beginners

Now try these!

- Yellow ribbon
- Pink flower
- Purple bird
- Gold flower vase
- Green mixing bowl
- Red candle
- Orange bird
- Blue flower
- Silver pitcher

Sleeping Beauty

While the thoughtful good fairies prepare for her birthday, Briar Rose visits with her forest friends. Look at the lovely gifts they've made her! Do you see them? And can you find some of her friends doing their part to make Briar Rose's sixteenth birthday so special?

Now try these!

◆ Skunk drummer
◆ Twirling squirrels
◆ Leaping lizard

◆ Fashionable turtle
◆ Bird quartet
◆ Juggling squirrel

◆ Jump-roping bunnies
◆ Bouquet-bearing raccoon
◆ Dressed-up snail

Beginners

Disney
Aladdin

Welcome to Agrabah! There's so much to see and do here, but Princess Jasmine has never been outside the palace walls. Look around the busy village for these residents going about their days. Then search for these items for sale here.

Beginners

Now try these!

- Surfboard
- Fancy necklace
- Jasmine doll
- Sword sandwich
- Empty treasure chest
- Basket of oranges
- Unusual underwear
- Soap
- Magic carpet

Aladdin

Princess Jasmine's single days are numbered! As the daughter of the Sultan, she must marry a prince by her next birthday. Many eligible princes have gathered to win her heart. Do you see them? Now look for some gifts they have brought to honor the princess.

I BATHE HOURLY

Now try these!

Beginners

- Gold statue of Jasmine
- Pegasus
- Chocolate statue of Jasmine
- Trojan horse
- Postage stamp of Jasmine
- Golden flower
- Painting of Jasmine
- New wardrobe
- Claw-foot bathtub

Aladdin

In the busy marketplace, Jasmine meets Aladdin. Jasmine thinks he is kind. Aladdin thinks Jasmine is beautiful . . . but he isn't sure about all these look-alikes! Can you spot them in the crowd? Then look for these strange marketplace things Jasmine has never seen before.

Beginners

Now try these!

Powerful mouse

Firebreather

Merchant who's all wet

Elephants in love

Swordfish slice

Bathing monkey

Goats sharing a snack

Snake doing the charming

Bookworm

Aladdin

Prince Ali has come to marry Jasmine. She doesn't know he is really Aladdin, transformed by the Genie's spell! Prince Ali's entrance parade is full of interesting things to look at. Can you find all of these performers, animals, and spectators in the street?

Beginners

Now try these!

- Bandaged sword thrower
- Elvis peacock
- Elephant Abu
- Jasmine look-alike
- The real Jasmine
- Hula-hooping boy
- Rodeo Genie
- Crocodile-headed bird
- Child Genie

Prince Ali

He's the Greatest!

OH MY!!

What a Prince!

SULTAN'S MAGIC CLEAN

OASIS: THIS EXIT

ICE MAN

WATCH YOUR SPEED!

Aladdin

Ready to soar through the skies on a magical carpet ride, Aladdin and Jasmine find themselves in a whole new world . . . of traffic. While they try to enjoy their ride, see if you can find these riders and carpets in the rush-hour traffic jam.

Beginners!

Now try these!

Genie carpet

Taxi carpet

Tow carpet

Dog catcher's carpet

Fire carpet

Ice carpet

Carpet sweeper

Traffic-copter carpet

Picnic carpet

Aladdin

Leaping lamp oil! Jafar has gotten his hands on the Genie's lamp, and now he is the Genie's master. While Aladdin battles Jafar, look around his palace for these unlucky visitors. Then see if you can find these strange things that amuse Jafar.

Beginners

Now try these!

Golden goose eggs

Angry gray cat

King snake

Rat Jafar

Mummy

Can of worms

ABC's of Evil book

Knitting spider

Portrait of himself

Snow White and the Seven Dwarfs

Snow White has just discovered a charming little cottage tucked away in the woods. It belongs to seven untidy Dwarfs! While Snow White and her animal friends start cleaning, look for all of these things that need to be put away.

Beginners

Now try these!

- Shovel
- Bucket
- Blue-rimmed bowl
- Lamp
- Flowered pitcher
- Shoe
- Orange-and-brown teacup
- Newly shined spoon
- Pink-and-yellow mug

Snow White and the Seven Dwarfs

Snow White has found her prince, and the Seven Dwarfs are so happy for her! Look around the cottage for seven of each of these items they have brought to celebrate. Then look around for some gifts Snow White has left for them!

Beginners

Now try these!

- Blue blanket
- Mirror
- Glasses case
- Teddy bear
- Handkerchief
- Bass guitar
- Purple pillow
- Gold star
- Accordion

POCAHONTAS

Grandmother Willow is a wise, ancient spirit. Pocahontas often visits her to seek her advice. The enchanted glade where Grandmother Willow lives looks empty... but things aren't always what they seem! Look around the forest to spot these objects that are not part of nature.

beginners

Now try these!

- Violin
- Bow
- Ear of corn
- Cup and saucer
- Spoon
- Watch
- Compass
- Fork
- Sword